#62
Lake View Terrace Branch
12002 Osborne Street
Lake View Terrace, CA 91342

OCT 0 7 2002

W9-CEL-666

Why the Chicken Crossed the Road

XZ
M

DAVID MACAULAY

Houghton Mifflin Company
Boston

For Tom Sgouros

Library of Congress Cataloging-in-Publication Data

Macaulay, David.
  Why the chicken crossed the road.

  Summary: By crossing a road, a chicken sets off a
series of wild events, in which the Anderson twins
blow up their bathroom and the brave young Hooper lad
is rolled up and delivered inside an Oriental rug.
  [1. Humorous stories] I. Title.
PZ7.M1197Wh   1987   [E]   87-2908
ISBN 0-395-44241-9

Copyright © 1987 by David Macaulay

All rights reserved. For information about permission
to reproduce selections from this book, write to
Permissions, Houghton Mifflin Company, 215 Park Avenue
South, New York, New York 10003.

Printed in the United States of America

RNF ISBN 0-395-44241-9
PAP ISBN 0-395-58411-6
BVG 10 9 8 7

Why the Chicken Crossed the Road

One day a chicken ran across a road.
This startled some cows, who stampeded
over an ancient bridge,

4

causing it to collapse onto a passing train.

Desperate Dan, who was being
taken to jail for stealing,
escaped from the train,
but not before helping
himself to the contents
of the safe.
As he disappeared into the woods,
his sack tore on some brambles,
and one by one, his ill-gotten gains
slipped through the hole.

Spotting a shiny gold watch,
a magpie swooped down
and scooped it up.
But time does not fly.

The watch was too heavy for the bird,
who dropped it into the Fletchers'
water tank, blocking the pipe.

9

On her way up the ladder to investigate, Mrs. Fletcher saw smoke rising from the train, but since she didn't see the train itself, she promptly called the fire department.

Napoleon Greasling, who was always practicing for the next fire, forgot to lower the ladder, so it snapped the electric line to the Zembo Ice Company.

Although picturesque, the results snarled traffic
and delayed Mrs. Anderson's return home.

Left to their own devices,
the Anderson twins turned to science

and substantially enlarged the bathroom.
Stunned by the explosion, Clarella Sweet conducted
a surprise inspection of Mel Toom's garbage truck.
Ordered to rest for a few days, she reluctantly gave
her nephew Rollo her ticket to the big game.

Because the game was televised, Lulu Thump,
the retired math teacher, happened to notice
Rollo Sweet in the crowd and suddenly recalled
his abominable behavior in school.

She made an important discovery while burying
the remains of her television in the garden.

On its way to the Institute for closer inspection,
Miss Thump's find traveled past Fern's Carpet Shop,
where Barney Fern became so distracted that he
inadvertently rolled up his careless assistant
in one of their finest Oriental rugs.

Which is how the Hooper lad came to be
delivered to the Clepcoe mansion.

Assuming young Hooper had smuggled himself
in to steal the famous Clepcoe jewels,
Thompson was about to call the police
when the frightened boy
leapt out the window,

sending Officer Goode and his men
flying into the hydrangeas.

Which is where, with the help of Hooper's lanky legs,
they captured Desperate Dan.

And so we come upon the train
taking Dan to jail for stealing.
It approaches an ancient bridge.
Across the road from the bridge is a restaurant

where
Officer Goode and his men,
Mr. and Mrs. Fletcher, Napoleon Greasling, Tiberius
Zembo, Mrs. Anderson and the twins, Rollo and Clarella
Sweet, Mel Toom, Lulu Thump, Barney Fern, and Thompson
are gathered for a luncheon to honor the brave young
Hooper lad, who orders chicken.

Which is why.